Timely
Umit Upturns
TIM

Mary Catherine Rolston

Illustrations by Keith Cains

◆ FriesenPress

Suite 300 - 990 Fort St
Victoria, BC, V8V 3K2
Canada

www.friesenpress.com

ISBN
978-1-5255-2365-6 (Hardcover)
978-1-5255-2366-3 (Paperback)
978-1-5255-2367-0 (eBook)

1. JUVENILE FICTION

Distributed to the trade by The Ingram Book Company

Dedication

To my Dear Friend Keith, who is trusting, tenacious and a tiger of courage and honour.

Outside Dalyan,
Turkey, lived
Timurhan,
a teeny turtle who was
called **Tim.**
He lived between a trail and
a creek where he would swim.
He was **timid, tender,
tolerant, thankful,
thoughtful** and always
told the **truth.**
He would go about his
business quietly and politely,
never being uncouth.
As a tremendous listener,
he had no thirst for talk.
He was a bit of a loner,
as shyness was his
stumbling block.

He **tenaciously** focused on tasks in a **trance**-like state.
He avoided others and stayed alone where he would hibernate.
Some animals **thought** he was a snob with a thorny mindset,
So they avoided him, **thinking** he was a **threat.**
Slowly but surely, **Tim** became rigid, always needing to be in control.
He did not share or surrender to others; he became like a gloomy troll.
This growing negativity insulated **Tim** in a vacuum of isolation.
Tim's solutions to problems lacked interaction or cooperation.

One day, a **thunderous** storm descended without warning. As Tim dove into the creek, darkness overtook the morning.

Torrential rains broke through the sky like a tear in a dark gray sheet. The heavy shower washed away the dust and thick, stifling heat.

Its stinging, pelting attack destroyed the
delicate and weak as it fell,
Filling streams and creeks until even the
rivers did swell.

A tsunami-like flow **transported Tim,** tossing, turning and twisting down stream. **Terrified** and **traumatized,** he choked away water. "HELP!" he screamed

After ten hours, **tides** deposited **trembling Tim** twenty 'K south of his home.

Shocked, he lay silent, exhausted, covered in a light white foam.

Lost in a dream-like state of neither here nor there,
he was tucked in his cozy shell.

A hot breeze rhythmically blew across his dome bringing
a slight gamey smell.

Poking his head out to explore, he felt a hairy rug warming his
soft underside.

Dazed and dizzy, his eyes finally flickered, opening wide.

His heart skipped a beat; he saw an endless furry striped rug
of orange and black.

This rug had a heartbeat, rising and falling. Then he heard
a lick and a smack.

Could this be? Was he resting on one of nature's mightiest beasts?

Would he become this creature's next appetizer or mini feast?

In seconds, he felt the damp, sandy **tongue** slowly roll across his roof.

Without hesitating, he popped into his shelled trailer home with a poof!

Hearing a muted **thump** as he **tumbled** off onto a bed of
spongy mud,

He now wondered why fate deliberately delivered him here after the flood.

Tim again mustered up courage. His pulse pattering, he poked out his
little head.

Seeing a large head with two glassy yellow eyes stirred feelings
of dread.

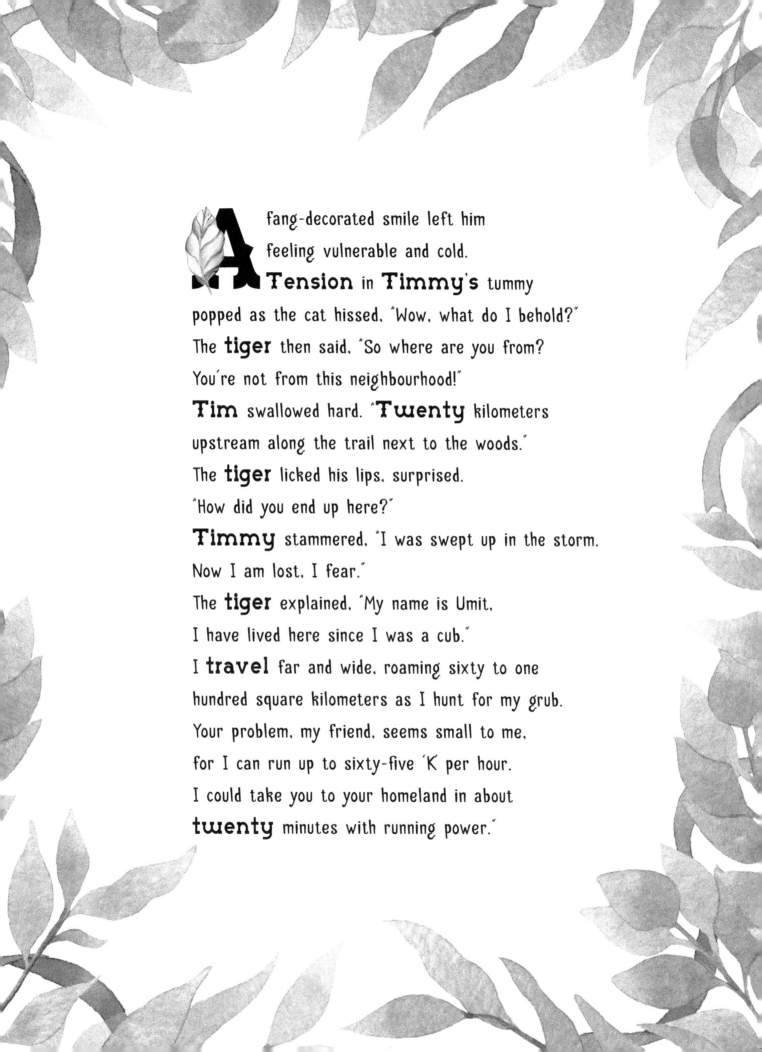

A fang-decorated smile left him
feeling vulnerable and cold.
Tension in **Timmy's** tummy
popped as the cat hissed, "Wow, what do I behold?"
The **tiger** then said, "So where are you from?
You're not from this neighbourhood!"
Tim swallowed hard. "**Twenty** kilometers
upstream along the trail next to the woods."
The **tiger** licked his lips, surprised.
"How did you end up here?"
Timmy stammered, "I was swept up in the storm.
Now I am lost, I fear."
The **tiger** explained, "My name is Umit,
I have lived here since I was a cub."
I **travel** far and wide, roaming sixty to one
hundred square kilometers as I hunt for my grub.
Your problem, my friend, seems small to me,
for I can run up to sixty-five 'K per hour.
I could take you to your homeland in about
twenty minutes with running power."

Tim thought long and hard. Gee, I could get a ride with this giant orange-striped kitty.

He does seem to be sincere; he's willing to show me kindness and some pity.

Then doubt did rise quickly like a tidal wave of pending doom—

Oh, can I trust him? He might eat me. I'll end up in my tomb!

Umit could see nervous beads of sweat on Tim's wrinkled brow.

"Tim, I do understand how you feel threatened right now. You may not believe this, but I myself have been threatened with death.

Humans are ruining the ecosystem, killing Caspian tigers, taking away our breath.

My friend, trust me, I have no interest in making you my afternoon snack.

You're too small to satisfy any hunger; you're not tantalizing me, making my lips smack.

Truly, I just want to help out a fellow creature of the earth in need."

Tim thought, Hmmm, Umit seems honest and willing to do this good deed.

"But how do I know you aren't lying or will trick me in the end?"

"**TIM!**" Umit roared in pure frustration, building fear in his new friend.

Umit then lowered his voice to a tender whisper. "I promise, I will keep my word.

Here's an idea, why don't you ride on my head; that might be preferred."

Tim's face lit up. Hmmm, I could surrender, have faith and hope. Riding on his head is a safe place, and I can hold onto his fur like a rope.

Taking a deep breath, Tim looked at Umit. "Okay, it's a deal." He smiled.

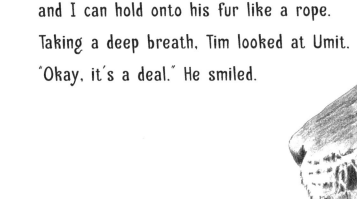

Slowly he crawled on top of Umit's head, looking like a cowboy in the wild.

Confidently, **Tim** yelled, "Onward home, my **transporter**, let us ride with the wind!"

They were off at warp speed, scarcely **touching** the **terrain**,

Tim's eyes bright as he grinned.

Tim had never seen the world from such a magnificent height and speed.

Awestruck wonder filled his heart,
while his need to be in control and
fear did recede.
As promised, Umit delivered **Tim** home in
what seemed like two shakes and a wink.

Upon arrival, the other animals stood in shock, rubbing their eyes with a blink.

Proudly, **Tim** crawled off Umit's head and down over his wet snout.

Umit rolled out his **tongue** while the animals watched in panic, ready to shout.

Courageously and confidently, **Tim** crawled from the orange and black carpet to the ground.

Tim turned to Umit and said, "**Thank** you, your influence on me has been profound."

Umit tenderly smiled, saying, "**Tim**, I **think** you have learned a thing or two about trust.

I get the sense that your fears have disintegrated into dust!"

"You are right, Umit. I feel free, and that negativity has been lifted.

Today I learned to see the world differently; **thankfully**, I have been gifted.

You have shown me how acts of kindness bring flexibility, faith, hope and joy.

Allowing the flowers of optimism and **trust** to bloom; fear has been destroyed."

So from that day on, **Tim** and Umit saw each other every Sunday afternoon. Umit became the transporter when local animals were displaced during monsoons. **Tim**'s shyness withered away; he became known as the great listener and sage. His **tenderness, tolerance** and **thoughtfulness** shone bright into his old age.

ind the **T** words in the story and learn the meaning of the more difficult words using the synonyms listed in red (these are words that have the same or almost the same meaning).

1. Turkey
2. Timurhan
3. teeny
4. turtle
5. Tim
6. trail
7. timid
8. tender - **loving**
9. tolerant - **easy going**
10. thankful
11. thoughtful
12. truth
13. tremendous - **huge**
14. thirst - **desire**
15. talk
16. tenaciously - **stubbornly**
17. tasks
18. trance – **dream-like or dazed**

19. thorny - **difficult**
20. threat - **danger**
21. troll
22. this
23. thunderous - **loud**
24. the
25. torrential – **overflowing or very heavy**
26. tear
27. thick
28. tsunami – **tidal wave or big flood**
29. tossing
30. turning
31. twisting
32. terrified - **scared**
33. traumatized – **distressed or shocked**
34. ten
35. tides

36. trembling - **shaking**
37. twenty
38. tucked
39. trailer
40. thump - **bang**
41. tumbled
42. two
43. tension – **stress or strain**
44. tummy
45. tiger
46. trail
47. travel
48. tidal - **huge**
49. trust
50. tomb
51. threatened - **in danger**
52. taking
53. tantalizing – **persuading or enticing**

54. truly - **really**
55. thought
56. trick
57. tender
58. transporter
59. touching
60. terrain - **land**
61. thank you
62. thing
63. today
64. thankfully
65. tenderness – **with love and care**
66. tolerance – **patience and guts**
67. thoughtfulness – **kindness**

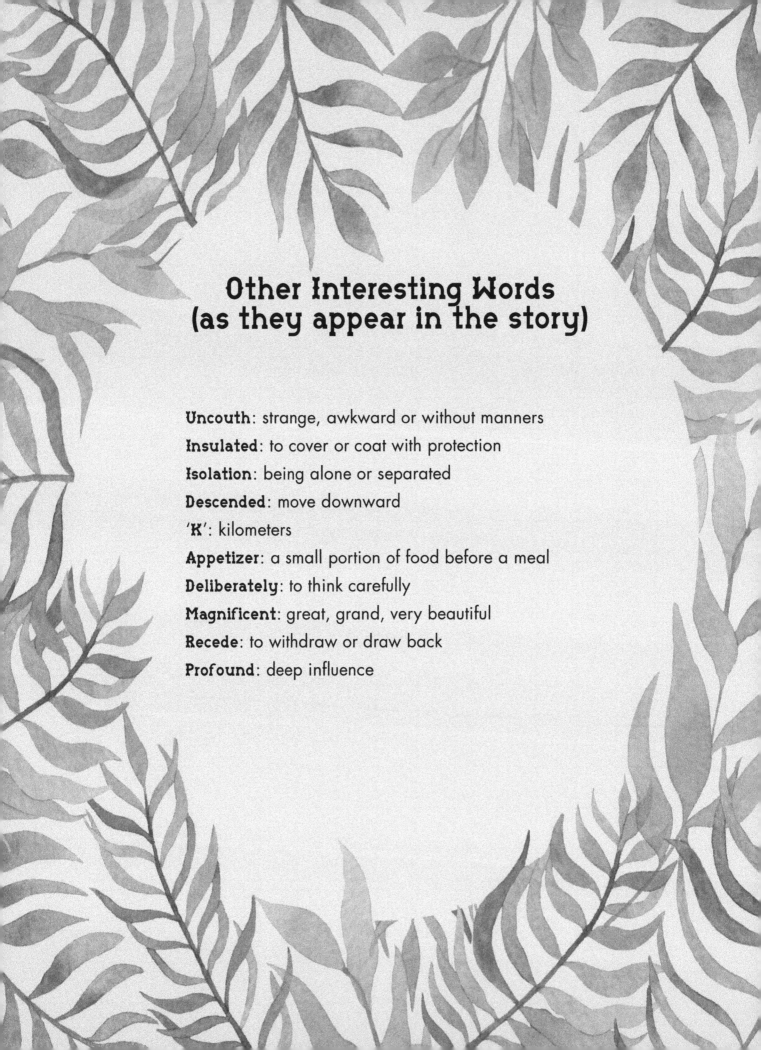

Other Interesting Words
(as they appear in the story)

Uncouth: strange, awkward or without manners

Insulated: to cover or coat with protection

Isolation: being alone or separated

Descended: move downward

'K': kilometers

Appetizer: a small portion of food before a meal

Deliberately: to think carefully

Magnificent: great, grand, very beautiful

Recede: to withdraw or draw back

Profound: deep influence

A Few Facts and Further Reading links:

The Caspian Tiger: As of the late 1970s, the Caspian tiger was considered extinct. Since then it has been determined that its genetic makeup is very similar to the Amur tiger. Consequently, the Kazakhstan government and the World Wildlife organization are working together to develop programs to reintroduce tigers to the Caspian region in Central Asia.

Further Reading: http://www.worldwildlife.org/species/tiger
http://www.worldwildlife.org/press-releases/
tigers-could-roam-once-more-in-central-asia
http://voices.nationalgeographic.com/2015/02/21/
is-extinct-forever-central-asias-caspian-tiger-traverses-the-comeback-trail/

The Nile Turtle or River Turtle: A soft-shelled, freshwater turtle. Its shell can reach a length of approximately a meter and it can weigh forty-five kilograms. It is primarily a carnivore, and it can swim under water for long periods of time. Due to heavy boating traffic along the Daylan River, the Nile turtle runs the risk of extinction. It is mainly a river turtle, but sometimes can be seen out at sea.
http://www.sustainabledalyan.webeden.co.uk/#/nile-turtle/4577267021

The Loggerhead Turtle: Further out along the seashores of the Iztuzu Beach, one can find this endangered turtle species. On average, these turtles can grow from seventy centimeters to a meter and weigh from eighty to two-hundred kilograms. They can live for more than fifty years and they are carnivores Although they are not endangered, they are vulnerable to being caught in fishing nets. They are essential to the sea-life ecosystem.
http://www.worldwildlife.org/species/loggerhead-turtle

2

5

Can You Name Tim's Friends?

2

3

1- Weasel

2- Squirrel

3- Shrew

4- Rat

5- Rabbit

6- Otter

5

1

4

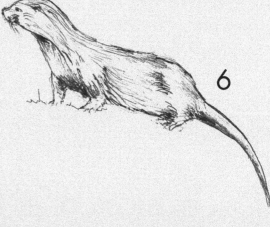

6

CPSIA information can be obtained
at www.ICGtesting.com
Printed in the USA
LVHW07s1202210518
577747LV00005B/2/P